# the cold little voice

ALISON HUGHES

illustrated by JAN DOLBY

CLOCKWISE
PRESS

Published by Clockwise Press Inc., 42 Sunbird Blvd, Keswick ON L4P 3R9

solange@clockwisepress.com
www.clockwisepress.com
10 9 8 7 6 5 4 3 2 1
Library and Archives Canada Cataloguing in Publication
Hughes, Alison, 1966-, author
The cold little voice / Alison Hughes ; [illustrated by]
Jan Dolby.
A poem.
ISBN 978-1-988347-11-0 (hardcover)
I. Dolby, Jan, illustrator  II. Title.
PS8615.U3165C65 2018          jC811'.6          C2018-905388-7

Data available on file
Interior design by Jacqueline Hudon
Printed in Canada by Friesens

Canada Council    Conseil des arts
for the Arts      du Canada

We acknowledge the support of the Canada Council for the Arts, which last year invested $153 million to bring the arts
to Canadians throughout the country.
Nous remercions le Conseil des arts du Canada de son soutien. L'an dernier, le Conseil a investi 153 millions de dollars
pour mettre de l'art dans la vie des Canadiennes et des Canadiens de tout le pays.

Vincent Van Gogh once said, "If you hear a voice within you say 'you cannot paint,' then by all means paint, and that voice will be silenced."

Even great artists have struggled with cold little voices. They whisper inside all of us. They make us question ourselves. They stop us from trying new things. And they sometimes make us forget all our good points.

This story is about silencing your cold little voice by being kind to yourself and being your own best friend. And being free to be you.

—Alison Hughes

for Kate - AH

for Noreen - JD

I have a cold little voice that follows me everywhere. And sometimes it perches on my shoulder, digs in its claws and whispers its cold little thoughts.

It's the warning voice
that cries,

"Too wobbly!
You're going to fall!"

It's the sneaky voice that says,

"You're going to look silly!"

It's the sly voice that whispers,

"Don't even try--
you're not good enough,"

even though you are,
and most of the time you know it.

The cold little voice says my front teeth are crooked, my favorite pants are too short, my ears stick out,

ridiculous

too thick

squint

stick out

crooked

ugly

too short

my coat is ugly, my eyes squint up when I smile, my eyebrows are too thick and my new haircut is ridiculous.

It points out that I bite my nails, laugh too loudly, trip when I run upstairs, talk too much, blush, cry too easily, make smacking sounds when I chew, sing off-key, get the hiccups too often, and have sloppy writing.

wrong            wrong

"I get it!" I wail, "I'm all wrong! Are you done?"

"No," the little voice says coldly. "You also run funny."

I plug my ears and say:
"I will not listen to you!" And I try not to.

But I do.
And soon, all I can hear
is the cold little voice.

So I stop talking so much or laughing so loudly. Or being silly. Or running.
I don't wear what I like, draw what I want, or sing or dance. Ever.

I just stop.
I become small and still and grey.
And not me.

But the cold little voice doesn't stop whispering. Now it says,

"Your shoulders droop and you don't smile enough and your hair is dull and you walk too slowly and you still bite your nails..."

And when it has crushed me, and worn me down to a small, grey nothing, I wonder: "Will it ever, ever stop?"

And another voice answers.
A voice I never even knew was deep inside me.

My voice says, "I've had enough.
I'm better than it thinks I am.
I'll <u>make</u> it stop."

So I start looking for warmth and happiness.
I cuddle with creatures who don't hear cold little voices.

I sit in a sunbeam. I look up at the blue, blue sky.

I look for people who like me the way I am.
People who help.

The cold little voice never whispers around them.

And if I'm alone, and the cold little voice starts sneering,
I won't ignore it.

I will pity it.

Because I know now that it is cold
because it has no warmth or happiness.

But I do.

It is little because the things it whispers about are very, very small.

But I'm not.

So I will hug it close, and warm it up, and soothe it and sing to it.

And it will grow into a big, warm, kind voice. A voice that says:

"You can do it!"
or "Who cares if it's silly -
you're having fun!"
or "Everybody makes mistakes!"

A voice that says,

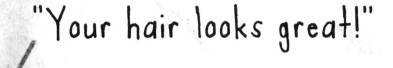

"Your hair looks great!"

"Your feet are exactly the right size!"

"Your crooked-tooth smile lights up your whole face!"

A voice that whispers proudly:

"You are special. You are unique."

And my warm, kind voice might make friends with other people's cold little voices.

Maybe one by one, they'll be warmed up.
And warmth and kindness and happiness
and silliness will spread...

And there will be no more cold little voices.

Even for people who run funny.